THIS **Elephant & Piggie** BOOK
BELONGS TO:

_____

_____

_____

To Eric, Bobbie and everyone at the Eric Carle Museum –
always worth the drive

Let's Go for a Drive!

An Elephant & Piggie Book

Mo Willems

WALKER BOOKS
AND SUBSIDIARIES
LONDON · BOSTON · SYDNEY · AUCKLAND

Piggie!

I have a great idea!

First, we need
a map.

I have
a map!

It might be sunny
while we drive.

I have the sunglasses!

ZAP!

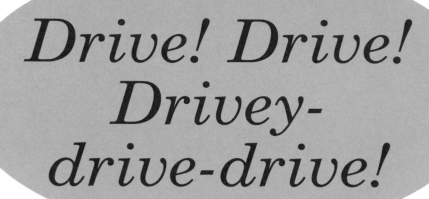

21

24

"Make a plan and stick to it" is what I say.

Read about Elephant and Piggie's other hilarious adventures in:

Mo Willems is the renowned author of many award-winning books,
including the Caldecott Honor winners *Don't Let the Pigeon Drive the Bus!*,
Knuffle Bunny and *Knuffle Bunny Too*. His other groundbreaking picture books
include *Knuffle Bunny Free, Leonardo, the Terrible Monster* and
Goldilocks and the Three Dinosaurs. Before making picture books,
Mo was a writer and animator on Sesame Street, where he won six Emmys.
Mo lives with his family in Massachusetts, USA.

Visit him online at **www.mowillems.com** and **www.GoMo.net**

This is a work of fiction. Names, characters, places and incidents are either
the product of the author's imagination or, if real, used fictitiously.

First published in Great Britain 2016 by Walker Books Ltd
87 Vauxhall Walk, London SE11 5HJ

First published in the United States by Hyperion Books for Children
British publication rights arranged with Wernick & Pratt Agency, LLC

2 4 6 8 10 9 7 5 3

© 2012 Mo Willems

The right of Mo Willems to be identified as author and illustrator of this work has been
asserted by him in accordance with the Copyright, Designs and Patents Act 1988

This book has been typeset in Century 725 and Grilled Cheese

Printed in China

British Library Cataloguing in Publication Data:
a catalogue record for this book is available from the British Library

ISBN 978-1-4063-7357-8

www.walker.co.uk